I AM EVERY GOOD THING

DERRICK BARNES

illustrated by

GORDON C. JAMES

Nancy Paulsen Books
An imprint of Penguin Random House LLC, New York

Visit us online at penguinrandomhouse.com

Library of Congress Cataloging-in-Publication Data
Names: Barnes, Derrick D., author. | James, Gordon C., illustrator.
Title: I am every good thing / Derrick Barnes; illustrated by Gordon C. James.
Description: New York: Nancy Paulsen Books, [2020] | Summary: Illustrations and easy-to-read text pay homage to the strength, character, and worth of a child.
Identifiers: LCCN 2019037091 | ISBN 9780525518778 (hardcover) | ISBN 9780525518785 (ebk) | ISBN 9780525518792 (kindle edition)
Subjects: CYAC: Self-confidence—Fiction. | Character—Fiction.
Classification: LCC PZ7.B26154 Iaak 2020 | DDC [E]—dc23
LC record available at https://lccn.loc.gov/2019037091

Manufactured in China by RR Donnelley Asia Printing Solutions Ltd.
ISBN 9780525518778
10 9 8 7 6 5

Design by Eileen Savage | Text set in Beaufort Pro
The illustrations were done with oil paints.

To Tamir Rice,
Trayvon Martin,
EJ Bradford,
Jordan Edwards,
Michael Brown,
Jordan Davis,
and Julian Mallory.
—D.B.

To my son, Gabriel,
and all little brothers like him.
—G.C.J.

I am
a nonstop ball of energy.
Powerful and full of light.
I am a go-getter. A difference maker.
A leader.

I am every good thing that makes the world go round.
You know—like gravity, or the glow of moonbeams
over a field of brand-new snow.

I am good to the core, like the center
of a cinnamon roll.

Yeah, that good.

I am skateboard tricks,
scraped knees and
elbows.

But you know what?
I am right back on
my feet again.

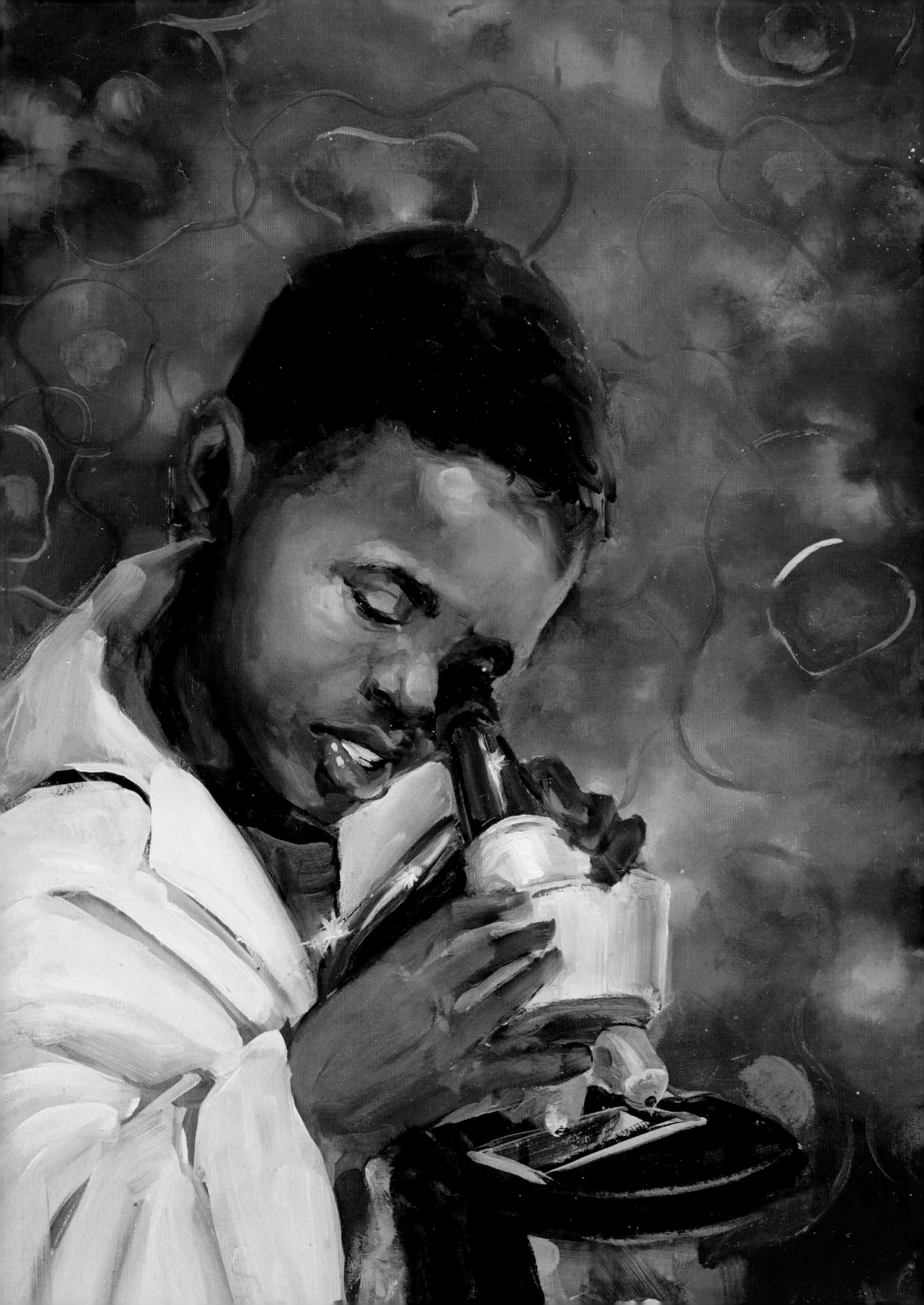

I am one eye open, one eye closed,
peeking through a microscope,
gazing through a telescope,
checking out the spaces
around me
and plotting out those far-off places
I have yet to go—but will.

I am a gentleman and a scholar.
I am kind and polite, like, “yes, ma’am,” and “yes, sir,”
helping my grandmother cross the street, and
saying “bless you” when a stranger
has to sneeze.

I'm a *coooooool* breeze.
A perfect paper airplane that glides
for blocks, for miles, forever.

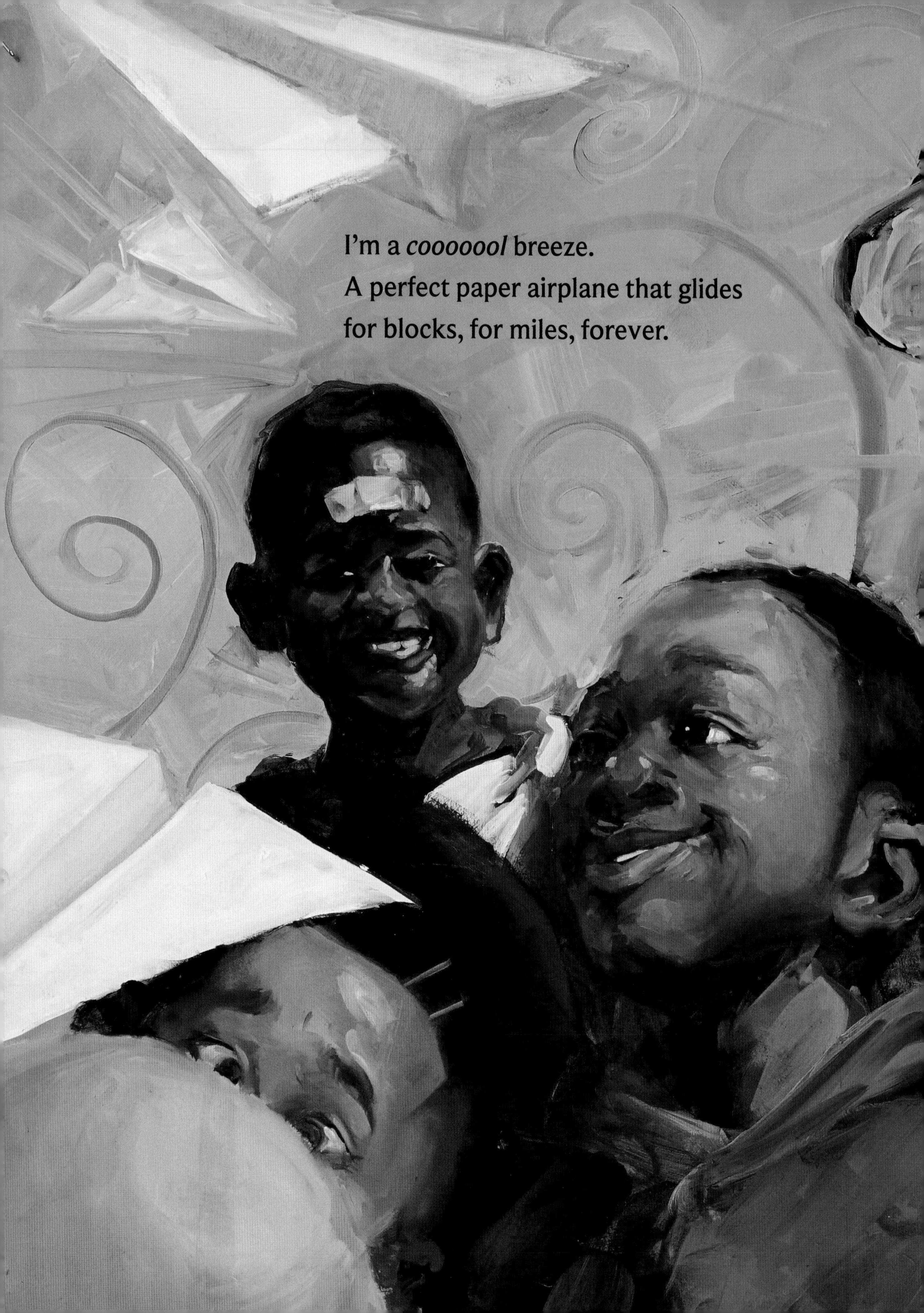

I am a roaring flame of creativity.
I am a lightning round of questions, and
a star-filled sky of solutions.
I am an explorer, planting a flag on every
square foot of this planet where I belong.
I am a sponge, soaking up information,
knowledge, and wisdom.
I want it all, and I am allllll ears.

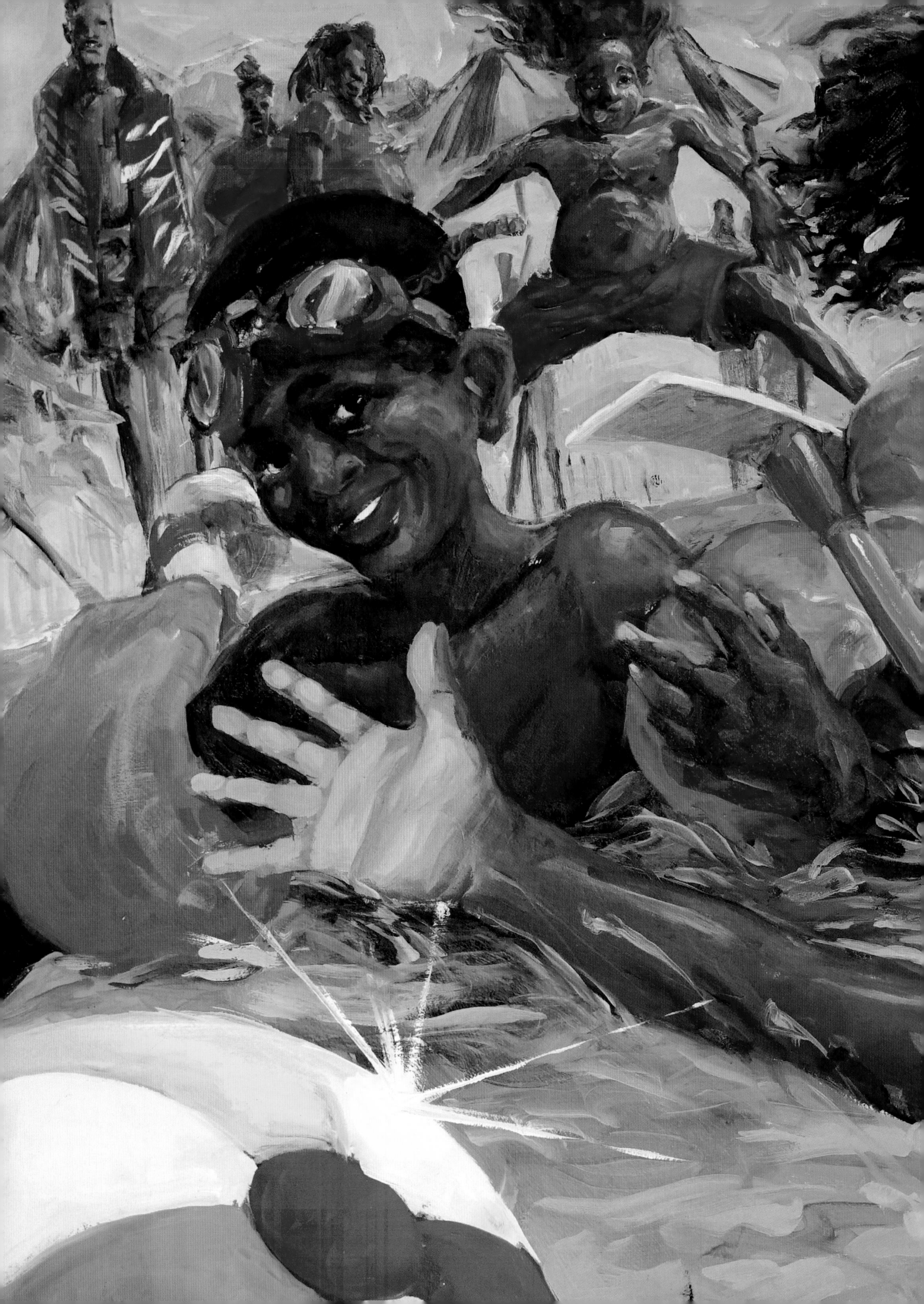

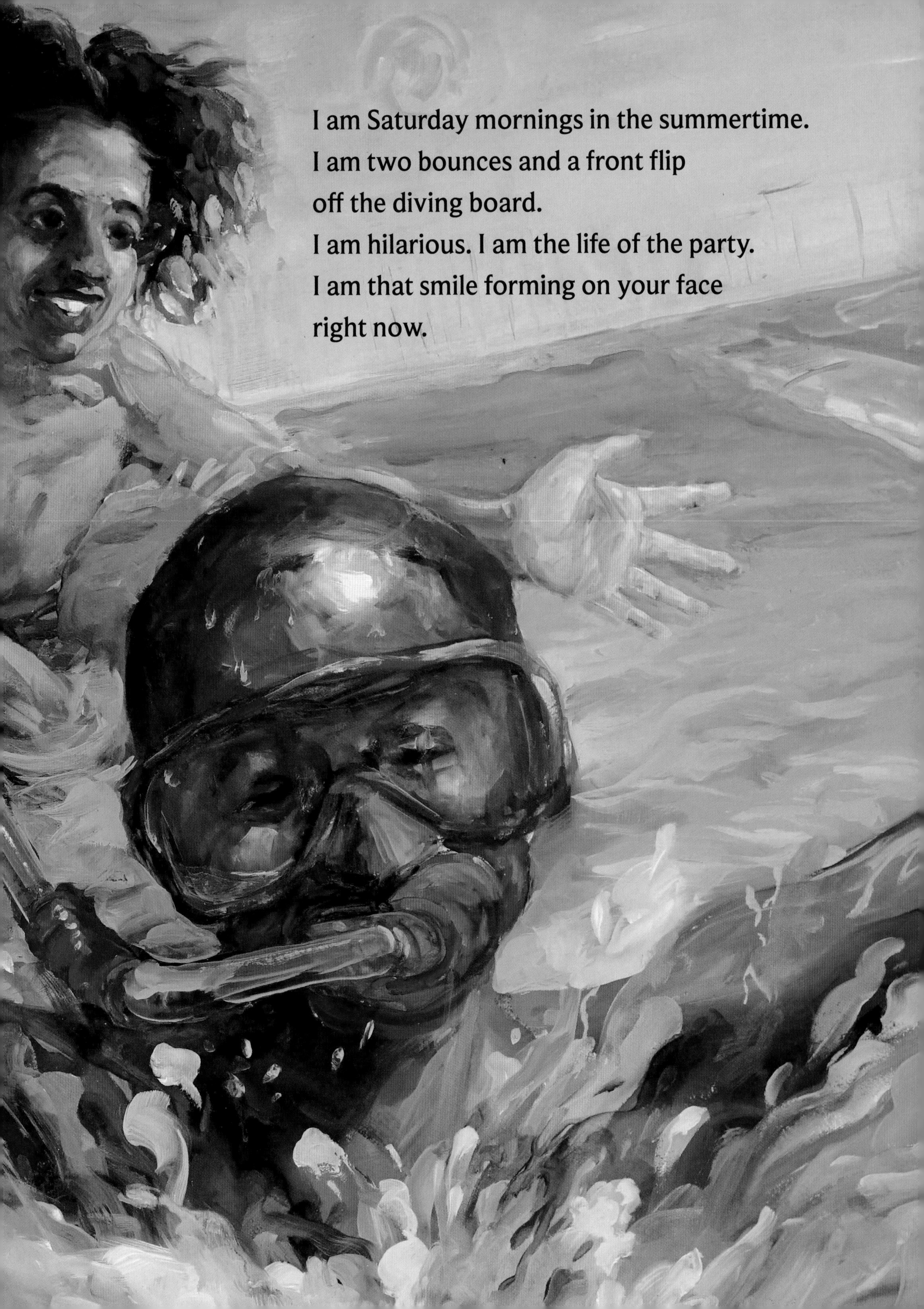

I am Saturday mornings in the summertime.
I am two bounces and a front flip
off the diving board.
I am hilarious. I am the life of the party.
I am that smile forming on your face
right now.

I'm the *BOOM-BAP—*
BOOM-BOOM-BAP
when the bass line thumps and the
kick drum jumps.
I'm the perfect beat, the perfect rhyme,
keeping everything on point and
always on time—
but you already knew that.

I am a grand slam,
bases fully loaded.
I'm a nasty two-handed dunk,
holding on to the rim,
just to remind you that
I'm still the man.
Believe that.

I am the undisputed champion.
I am a highlight reel of magnificence.
I am the celebration, the applause,
and the standing ovation.
I am victory.

I am a brother,
a son,
a nephew,
a favorite cousin,
a grandson.
I am a friend.
I am real.

I am tight hugs, a hand
to hold, a shoulder to cry
on—if you have to.
I hope you never have to.
I am here.

Although I am something like a superhero,
every now and then,
I am afraid.

I am not what they might call me,
and I will not answer to any name
that is not my own.
I am what I say I am.

I am that sound in the forest when the mighty tree falls.

I am waves crashing gently on the shore.
I am a force of nature. A miracle. A blessing.

I am brave. I am hope.
I am my ancestors' wildest dream.

I am worthy of success,

of respect, of safety, of kindness, of happiness.

And without a shadow
of a doubt,
I am worthy
to be loved.

I am worthy
to be loved.